A DEMON'S CHRISTMAS

A SHORT CHRISTMAS ROMANCE

❄

STACY JONES
K.B. EVERLY

After centuries of feeling alone, Krampus' favorite demon, Holly, has decided to change the rules.

On Christmas Eve, when the demons are let loose to capture human prey, Holly finds three men who fit the sacrificial bill. Little does she know the violent Vien, the guilty Nash, and the sad Grey are everything she needs to escape the loneliness of her long existence.

With midnight coming fast and the arrival of Krampus imminent, Holly must decide if she should do her job and throw the men to the depths of Krampus' hell, or ask her master for one gift.

To make a demon's Christmas wish come true.

CHAPTER ONE

❄

*H*olly stepped out of the car and breathed in the cold winter air, taking in all the scents around her with a slight grimace. She loved the yearly excursions she and her demon brethren made to the humans' dimension, but the stench got tiresome very quickly. She much preferred the brimstone smell of home.

Shaking out her long, dark red hair, she adjusted her top. As always, on hunting night, she was dressed to kill in a tight, black corset paired with equally tight, leather pants and black, thigh-high boots. Despite the frigid temperatures, she didn't need a coat. Demons didn't feel the cold.

Shutting the car door, she stalked to the rundown, single-story building and entered, letting the delicious scents of depression and misery wash over her. Grinning hungrily, she scanned the room, taking in the dim lighting, the sad music playing on the jukebox, and the smattering of men all staring blankly into their drinks.

She'd learned how to hunt smart over the centuries

and knew these bars always held the prey she coveted. After all, only the sad and lonely spent Christmas Eve in such a place, and it was exactly those people Krampus liked best. Well, they were actually the ones *she* liked best, but Krampus appreciated her tastes. That mutual love of broken souls was how Holly came to be his favorite—a status she enjoyed immensely and reaffirmed every year by bringing him the choicest victims.

It was her job to lure them in, then feed their souls to her master. Krampus kept the tastiest souls for himself but threw the vast majority into The Pit to power the Underworld for another year. This was a never-ending cycle. Every year, the gates opened on Christmas Eve and the demons were allowed to prowl for another batch of souls to sustain them.

Holly walked to the bar, peering closely at every man present as she went, and searched for the ones that smelled just right. She took a deep breath, filtering through the different emotions permeating the room.

There.

Her gaze cut to a man seated a few feet down the bar. He was handsome: at least six feet, muscular, with blonde hair cut short in what she recognized as a military style. He glanced over at her, checking her out with a kind of detached appreciation, letting her see the rest of him. He had cornflower blue eyes and a masculine face full of angles, only softened by his full lips.

Her nostrils flared as she took another breath of him. Guilt, remorse, shame, hate. So complex, so delightfully damaged.

Delicious. Yes, he'll do nicely.

"What'll you have, ma'am?" the bartender asked.

Turning, Holly saw he'd directed his question at her chest. More specifically, the pale mounds of her breasts. She eyed him up and down, then sniffed the air around him. Her face screwed up at the eager desperation pouring off of him. She snorted inelegantly to rid her nose of the stench that suffocated the delicious scent of the other man.

"Bourbon. Neat," she clipped, wanting him to step away and take his disgusting desperation with him.

Dismissing his affronted look, she pivoted away and leaned back against the bar top. Her gaze landed on a man seated in the farthest corner, shrouded in darkness. He tasted like blood and violence, but there was loneliness there too. Holly narrowed her eyes to pierce the shadows, taking in his buzzed, black hair, striking features, and cold, blue eyes. Breathing deeper, she caught the distinct scent of a sociopath coming from him.

Mmm, my favorite. You'll be victim number two.

The door opened, drawing her attention as a gust of frigid air and the smell of depression, heartache, and fresh sorrow blew in. Holly followed him with her gaze as the man emitting those emotions entered, then took a seat at a booth on the far side of the bar.

He was plain in almost every way. He had medium, brown hair that was cut in a reasonably stylish fashion— long enough to grip in her fist, but not so long as to look unkempt—average height at about five-foot-eleven, watery blue eyes, and attractive, though not overly so. He was someone you wouldn't look at twice on a crowded street, someone easily forgotten. But not for Holly. She could taste the abundance of misery pumping from him like a river, exceptional in its intensity and richness. His sorrow was divine.

Victim number three. Now, to lure them in...

There were a few other men who tasted nice, but she was putting her money on those three. They all had the underlying scent of surrender, which meant they were ready to let go. Ready to leave this place in any way possible, whether physically or spiritually.

Holly reached back for her drink and took a sip, eyeing her prey over the rim as she unleashed her pheromones. Setting the glass back down with a soft clink, she took a lap around the room, spreading her essence. She could sense it infecting the men as their lust became thick in the air, but only those ready to move on from this world would feel any desire to actually approach her.

She stepped onto the small dance floor and flicked her fingers, changing the music on the jukebox from a slow melancholy tune to something with a beat, something that sounded like sex and darkness. Tipping her head back, she bit her lip and swayed, letting the bass guide her movements.

Within a minute, she felt them approach. Holly dropped her head back down and opened her eyes to slits. The one leaking delicious depression, the one drenched in violence and sin, and the one that tasted of guilt and shame were making their way toward her.

Damn, I'm good.

CHAPTER TWO

a smile curled her blood red lips as she eyed the dark one. He was big, at least six-foot-four, and brawny. At five-eight, not many humans could tower over her, but he did. Spinning away when he came close, she leaned back and undulated against him as she watched the other two draw near.

Her smile grew when she felt the dark one feather his fingers down her sides until he could grip her hips. He was surprisingly gentle for being so soaked in bloodshed.

His name is Vien.

Now that she was touching him, she could see his life. He had a terrible childhood—raised with the kind of brutality even a demon such as her wasn't used to seeing —and his adulthood hadn't been any better. He'd been working for the Russian mob for over a decade now, doing their dirty work. Vien liked it—enjoyed the blood and pain—but he was lonely.

He thought no one could love a monster like him.

That knowledge sent a pang through her and made the

enticing sway of her hips stutter for a moment, before she recovered. She knew what it was like to yearn for acceptance, to want so badly for someone to love you—all of you—not just the pretty parts. Even demons had hearts and wanted to feel the warmth of devotion from another. And she hadn't felt even a speck of that kind of devotion in more years than she could count.

She stepped away from Vien and into the arms of the muscular blonde one plagued with guilt so thick, it was bittersweet on her tongue. She ran a hand up his square jaw, covered with a five o'clock shadow, then into his short hair.

Nash.

His guilt was the kind no man could ever come back from. It was the guilt of killing the one he loved more than anything—his wife.

They were high school sweethearts, inseparable since the moment they laid eyes on each other. Nash developed a drinking problem after the loss of their first-born child.

Too much of a problem.

Six years ago, he drove himself and his wife, pregnant with their second child, off a bridge and into a river after one too many drinks. She drowned. He didn't. He became detached from life and barely left his house unless going to work at a dead-end job that was on the brink of firing him.

She'd make him forget. At least for a little while. She leaned forward and licked the corner of his full lips, gaining a hungry groan from him. She smiled wickedly and pushed back from him, landing in the arms of the third victim she'd chosen.

Grey.

He was hopeless. His blue eyes were bloodshot and watery from days of what she knew was crying. She slid her hands beneath the hem of his white, polo shirt, and was pleasantly surprised to feel a lovely six pack hidden beneath the oversized material. It was impressive for someone who looked so ordinary.

She scratched her nails down his flesh, then grabbed his hips to rock his pelvis into hers. She moved against him, sighing with bliss as the other two closed in behind her.

She leaned forward and nipped at Grey's neck, sucking at the salty skin there. His life flashed before her in quick succession.

His immense sadness bled through her system, igniting her never ending hunger for the broken and desolate. He had walked in on his fiancé just a week before, fucking another man in their bed. One who was apparently twice as rich as he was. They were due to be married in three weeks. Grey didn't get angry. No, he turned off every emotion except the sadness and wallowed in it. He sulked. He stopped eating or sleeping. He just wanted to forget. Holly reveled in the tears that painted his face and the misery that allowed her to lure him in.

They were all hers now.

She fisted his locks and pulled his mouth down hard on hers, feasting on his kiss like a demon starved.

GREY WAS NEVER THE TYPE TO THROW HIMSELF AT ANYONE.

Yet, as desperately as he still wanted his ex-fiancé when he walked into the bar, she was all but a dream the second his gaze landed on the red headed woman now kissing him with a hunger he'd never experienced.

He wanted to do things to this woman he'd never done with his fiancé.

He wanted to kneel at her feet, to worship her, to offer her anything and everything she wanted, be it his body, mind, or soul. He wanted to be *hers.* Images of her pinning him down and taking what she wanted flashed through his mind, and he loved every second.

A HAND SLID ALONG HOLLY'S EXPOSED STOMACH, MAKING her break contact with Grey. She turned and looked up into the calculated eyes of her sociopath, Vien. He wanted her lips as well. Badly. She'd dare say he'd even kill for a kiss.

While she wasn't against a little murder here and there, she wanted his mouth on hers just as much and she wasn't in the habit of denying herself anything she wanted. She pressed herself against him, but barely had time to smile before he dove at her. He lifted her up until the tips of her boots were barely touching the floor, then licked teasingly at her lips, methodical and coaxing as he asked her to open for him. Holly wanted to see that control break. She wanted to taste the chaos locked away inside him. She sensed it, begging to be freed so it could rain terror on the world.

· · ·

VIEN WAS USED TO ALWAYS BEING IN CONTROL, USED TO keeping the monster inside him on a short leash and only letting it peek out when he killed someone. But the woman in his arms made him feel reckless. She made him feel need—desire—so strong it made his control slip.

The longer he kissed her, the less he cared about restraining himself. Something whispered that, maybe with her, he could reveal the true darkness hiding inside him. That small, emaciated voice of hope wondered if she might be the one to look upon him and smile, to not run screaming if he showed her what he hid. Vien didn't even know her fucking name and, yet, he wanted to bare his soul to her. He wanted to let her see his monster more than he'd ever wanted anything.

He wanted to be *hers.*

HOLLY COULD FEEL THE DEMANDING PULSE OF anticipation from the guilty one, Nash, beside her, even over Vien's sharp lust. She could sense the countdown happening in his mind, ticking away before he gave up trying to be patient and snatched her into his arms.

Mmm, a bit of dominance in that one.

It was hard, but she managed to pull herself away from Vien's hungry lips. She spun herself completely away from him and Grey, so she could lavish in the attention Nash wanted to give her.

NASH DIDN'T TRY TO TEMPER THE STRENGTH OF HIS GRIP when he yanked the red-headed woman to him, nor did he soften the fury of his kiss as he dove at her. He hadn't touched a woman in so long, hadn't wanted to... not until he'd seen *her*.

Hands bruisingly tight on her hips, he held her to him and bit her lip. In an instant, his constant guilt changed to anger—anger she'd broken through the shroud of sorrow he wore like a second skin, anger she was making him feel need, want, when the only thing he should feel was horror.

At the first forceful thrust of his tongue into her mouth, the anguish that never left him, diminished. It felt like nothing else could exist while he was touching her, like she was burrowing inside him and feasting on the endless pool of torment and heartache he carried. Even the memory of his dead wife's smile felt faint, distant. All he saw was *her*, this vixen who returned his punishing kiss with an aggression that far surpassed his own.

He wanted more. He wanted to hurt her. He wanted to fuck her. He wanted to fill her with the rage and pain that plagued him until he was empty, until everything that made him *him* was hers, until *he* was hers.

NASH'S GRIP WAS TIGHT WHEN HE YANKED HER AGAINST him, and his kiss was greedy, rough. He bit her lip, then forced her mouth open with the bold thrust of his tongue.

So much yummy anger in this one.

Growling, she bit him back, hard enough that she tasted blood. Instead of pulling away, Nash grunted low in his throat and kissed her harder.

Holly grinned against his bloody lips and coiled her

arms around his neck, pulling him with her as she backed into the other two. They pressed close until she could feel all of them against her.

They touched her, stroking her skin and unknowingly gifted her with images of their lives, flooding her with their dark emotions. She gloried in the pain they bled. They continued swaying to the music, falling deeper under her spell.

THEY STAYED LIKE THAT THROUGH ONE SONG, THEN another—grinding, swaying, and kissing—but something strange began to happen the more they touched her. She saw more of them, felt deeper inside them, past the surface of their emotions. There was a depth to each man, a complexity she found both intoxicating and dangerously alluring. That depth called to her in a way no one had in centuries.

Holly tried to shake off the fascination she could feel herself developing for them. They weren't for her, and she needed to remember that. These three perfect, delicious, intriguing men were for Krampus. She knew he would love them. This was one of the many reasons she was Krampus' favorite. She always brought the best souls to him, the fastest. He would be so proud, and maybe even reward her for this particularly solemn bunch she'd nabbed.

She just had to convince herself she wanted to hand them over.

CHAPTER THREE

✻

*H*olly managed to pull away from the guys and their sex fueled haze long enough to coral them outside.

They followed without question, drunk on her pheromones. She led them around to the alley beside the bar where a jet black, Rolls Royce Phantom limousine waited.

She grinned and walked to it. Opening the back door, she turned to the men, eyeing them alertly in case one of them decided to run. It had happened in the past. Sometimes, when her prey regained a bit of their senses, their survival instinct kicked in and undid all her hard work.

She always caught the runners, so it was more of a sting to her pride than an actual inconvenience. But, as she stared at the three men in front of her, she had the uncomfortable realization that she didn't want them to run. Not because she would have to chase them, but because she wanted them to *want* to go with her. Another realization followed on the heels of the first. If one of them did flee, she wasn't sure she would stop them.

Grey, Nash, and Vien all had more awareness in their eyes now that she wasn't touching them and they weren't enclosed in the building flooded with her essence, but none of them looked ready to flee. In fact, each of them, even the submissive Grey, appeared as if they were seriously contemplating snatching her up and getting her out of that dark alley. Holly could feel the need to protect her pumping off them in a warm stream. She felt her tiny, black heart swell in her chest, and clenched her teeth to hold back the disgustingly sweet smile that wanted to curl her lips.

Stop it, Holly. Do not get attached to the sacrifices. Doesn't matter if their emotions taste like ambrosia, or if they're sweet and yummy, or if each of them perfectly fits a part of you like a puzzle piece. They're not yours, and they never will be.

Holly shut off the instant spark of denial those thoughts caused and pushed them down, until she couldn't hear the seductive whisper telling her to find new victims and keep these for herself. Krampus would know and take them anyway.

"Come with me, and I'll show you the time of your lives," she repeated the line she used every year, holding out a hand. But this time, her grin was half-hearted at best and lacked its usual hunger.

Nash looked at her, searching her face for a moment like he could sense her sudden reluctance. Realizing she'd either accidentally broadcast her feelings, or he was becoming clear-headed enough to be more perceptive than she wanted, Holly stepped up to him and pulled him

15

down for a kiss. She sighed into his mouth, breathing her pheromones into him. When she pulled away, she could see the haze clouding his eyes again. She relaxed slightly when he slid into the car without further hesitation.

Walking to Vien next, she reached up to grip his chin, bringing his watchful eyes back to her. He bent readily when she tilted her face up, and took her lips in a hungry kiss, cupping her cheeks and sucking her bottom lip. She fell into him and damn near forgot to exhale her essence but remembered just as he began to pull away. His eyes were glazed when he blinked them open to stare down at her, then he too entered the car without pause.

Holly turned to Grey next. She saw his gaze, narrowed and suspicious, bouncing from her to where the other two were now seated in the Phantom. She tensed, sure he was going to run. Instead, he did something that shocked her. He relaxed and stepped closer, but rather than kissing her on her lips so she could drug him, he stared down at her for a second, then bent and pressed a soft kiss to her cheek.

When he straightened, he asked quietly, "What's your name?"

Holly could feel the interest coming from the other two and knew they'd heard his question. She wasn't in the habit of giving her name to her victims, but then again, they never asked. Between their own readiness to let go of this world, her pheromones, and the sense of lust and safety she instilled in them, there wasn't usually room for curiosity.

She opened her mouth, but instead of enthralling him as she had the others, her name slipped out.

"Holliarepzus."

She went perfectly still at hearing her full demon name escape. Her eyes went wide, and her heart began to pound. She'd only meant to tell him her human name.

Holly spun away and quickly got into the car, leaving Grey to follow if he wanted. She'd just done something she couldn't take back. By telling them her true name, she'd just created a bond between them—a bond that couldn't be broken.

They were hers now. And she was theirs.

Krampus is going to skin me alive.

CHAPTER FOUR

✳

*H*olly wasn't surprised when Grey got in behind her, not now that she'd foolishly tied them to her. She sat between him and Vien on the spacious backseat, with Nash on the far side, and stared blankly ahead while trying to work out how she was going to fix the mess she'd just created. Which might've been easier if she actually regretted what she'd done. But under the shock and burgeoning panic, was a sense of relieved satisfaction.

For the next hour at least, she wasn't alone.

For being such a long-lived race, demons courted in fast forward. After all, you didn't need weeks and months to get to know someone when you could see their lives in an instant and taste their true emotions on your tongue. Creating a bond between demons was done with a blood exchange, but with mortals, all you needed was to tell them your true name. It was rare that a demon tied a human to them, but not unheard of. Of course, it wasn't with victims specially picked out as a sacrifice for Krampus. *That* was unheard of.

With them all settled, and the door shut, the car purred to life and the lower demon in the driver's seat turned to face Holly.

"To the hotel, milady?" came Grug's gravelly voice.

"Hmm? Oh, yes. Take us to the hotel," she responded absentmindedly.

Holly wrinkled her nose at the slight putrid smell wafting off the creature, and at the sight of his human skin suit not quite fitting him right.

Lower demons like him served the higher demons of Krampus' legion. They were hideous and didn't have the power to take on appealing human forms. Instead, they would find a human, devour their insides, then parade around in their skin as they helped the higher demons with their soul seeking tasks.

This one was named Grug, and he'd been Holly's servant for the better part of a millennia.

When she noticed Grug's glowing, red eyes flash with nervousness, she smiled softly to reassure him. She hoped he hadn't heard her little slip, but she knew that was unlikely, particularly with the look he was giving her. Lower demons usually had very good hearing, all the better to listen to their masters.

She could see the apprehension in Grug's scarlet eyes, but she just shook her head, telling him not to say anything. If he didn't say anything, she could pretend he didn't know. He was unfailingly loyal to her, but Krampus didn't like disobedience and had a plethora of methods with which to make someone reveal their secrets. She didn't want Grug paying for her impulsiveness.

❄

THEY SPENT THE BEGINNING OF THE RIDE IN SILENCE, ONLY broken when Nash asked where they were going.

"To a holiday celebration. You'll be my guests," she answered, keeping it intentionally vague.

She could feel their curiosity grow at her announcement, and almost released a rush of pheromones to calm them back down to docility but stopped at the last second.

Turning, she gazed at each of them for a long moment, taking in the intensity in Nash's cornflower blue eyes, Vien's wary curiosity underlaid with almost violent determination, and the calm devotion coming from Grey.

They feel the bond, too.

Holly hadn't been sure if they would. She'd never told a human her name, so hadn't known if what she felt would be one-sided. Feeling what they felt meant she knew, without doubt, they were now as tied to her as she was to them.

There was a better than good chance Krampus would end up taking them from her, which meant she had two choices—waste time with worrying or enjoy what time they had left.

Holly had been alone for such a long time. If she only had them for a little while longer, she wanted memories to keep her company after they were gone.

That time, the rush of pheromones that left her were unintentional and caused a different reaction. She heard

Vien growl, while Nash groaned, and Grey released a shuddering sigh.

"Mine," she hissed.

"Yours," they answered as one, voices instantly rough with need.

Nash and Grey both began stripping out of their clothes while she moved to straddle Vien. Grinding down on the erection she could already feel straining his jeans, Holly attacked his mouth, delighted when he met her onslaught with equal fervor.

Nash's hands came around to remove her corset then returned with Grey's, both of them stroking her back and sides before they simultaneously cupped her breasts. Holly moaned into Vien's mouth when Grey gently brushed his thumb over her nipple while Nash pinched her other roughly. The disparity in their touch set her body alight.

Vien gripped her hips tighter, pulling her down on his lap, then tore his lips from hers to kiss and bite the column of her neck. Holly tipped her head back and closed her eyes, panting through blood red lips as they all touched her.

"Now," she breathed, lust and urgency ridding her of what little patience she had.

Dropping her head down, she pushed Vien against the back of the seat and tore his shirt open, then ran her sharp nails across his pecs. He pushed his hips up off the seat, lifting her with him, and shoved his jeans down, letting his long, thick shaft spring free and slap against the deliciously defined muscles of his abdomen.

Sighing in both lust and longing, Holly wiggled out of

her leather pants then straddled him again. Fisting his cock, she raised up on her knees and rubbed him teasingly against her wetness, watching his cold, blue eyes flare with heat. Vien's hands tightened on her hips, but to her surprise, he didn't shove her down over him.

Grinning devilishly at his control, Holly tormented him, sinking down just enough for him to enter her, only to lift up again when he tensed with expectation. She wanted to see his restraint snap, wanted the monster hiding behind his eyes to come out and play.

She watched Vien try valiantly to hold onto that control, before his gaze narrowed and his lip curled in a warning snarl. He slid his hands up to her waist, clenched them to hold her tightly, then pulled her down hard, impaling her on his cock. Holly cried out at the almost painful pleasure that tore through her, relishing in the burning stretch of his unmerciful entry.

She didn't give him time to recover his restraint, but immediately began riding him, fucking him so hard the slap of skin-on-skin nearly drowned out the sound of their moans.

Her orgasm built swiftly, beginning as tingles in her fingers and toes. Sinking her nails into the thick muscles of his shoulders, she rode him faster, then screamed when it hit. The streetlights streaming past looked like golden fireworks behind her closed lids, reflecting back her pleasure with their bright glow.

Vien let out a choked groan when her walls clamped down around him and pulled her down hard, shoving his cock as deeply inside her as possible. Buried to the hilt, he came, flooding her with his release.

Holly sucked in a shaky breath when the spasms slowed, and opened her bright, green eyes to slits to gaze down at him.

"You're mine, now. My Monster," she panted, rocking against him as she felt the last of his orgasm pumping inside her.

"Yes, my *koroleva*," he groaned, bliss and reverence overflowing from him in an exquisite torrent.

CHAPTER FIVE

※

*L*eaning down, Holly kissed Vien softly, lovingly, but Nash broke in and cut it short. He was done waiting. She gasped when he lifted her hips, roughly dragging her off of Vien's still hard cock.

He pulled her back, so her knees were barely holding her on the edge of the seat, then pushed her down with a hand between her shoulder blades, making her catch herself against the seat and tipping her ass up at the same time. He gave her no warning, slamming his thick cock inside her hard enough to force a cry from her throat and send her falling into Vien.

She felt him bend over her back, before his low, harsh voice whispered in her ear, "My turn."

Laughing with delight, she turned to look at him from inches away. His pretty, blue eyes were wild and the glint of cruelty in them excited her. Tilting her hips up, she flicked her tongue out and licked his lips provokingly.

"Fuck me, my Beast. Show me all that yummy anger

you've been hiding for so long," she breathed, then pushed her ass back into him.

That was all he needed to let go. Straightening, he fisted one hand in her long red hair and held her hip bruisingly tight with the other, then did exactly what she demanded—he fucked her with a ferocity she'd never experienced in all her long years. And she loved it.

Holly swayed against Vien, her entire body moving with the force of Nash's thrusts. She took his lips in a kiss, feeding him her moans and cries and shoved herself back harder, taking Nash deeper.

"Fuck, yes. Take my cock, Holly," Nash growled.

With the speed and power of his thrusts it wasn't long before they were both nearing the edge. He pounded into her harder, faster, then threw his head back and roared as he filled her with his release. Holly tore her mouth from Vien's to scream her pleasure, but her orgasm seized her throat, making her cry a silent one as every muscle in her body locked up.

While the last pulses of her release were still firing through her, Nash pulled out and moved to collapse on the seat beside Vien. Holly slid down to kneel on the floorboard and took in the sight of two of her men, naked and panting.

Feeling a surge of anticipation from Grey, she slowly turned her head and pinned him with her gaze, loving the way his pupils swelled, swallowing the watery blue of his eyes. Vien and Nash may be spent, but demons were made of sterner stuff and she was more than ready to take her pleasure from Grey.

Dropping down to her hands, she crawled across the

spacious floorboard to where he knelt. She scanned his body as she went, pleasantly surprised at the hard, defined muscles that covered him and the tantalizingly thick cock that stood proudly erect between his legs.

"Get on the seat, my Pet," she purred, cutting her eyes to the rear facing bench seat behind him.

Grey moved eagerly to sit down then watched her slow approach avidly. Holly zeroed in on the moisture beading on the head of his cock, feeling her mouth water when it spilled over and ran down the length of him.

She came to a stop between his knees and help his gaze as she lightly ran her tongue up his swollen shaft, collecting that wetness. She grinned at the shiver that ran through him and the way his eyes rolled into the back of his head.

While his eyes were closed, she turned her head and sank her teeth into the flesh of his inner thigh. She didn't bite him hard enough to break the skin, but it would definitely leave a mark. Grey's eyes sprang open and a hiss that anyone else would think was a sound of pain escaped him, but she knew better. She'd seen inside his soul and knew his darkest desires. She knew he craved to be dominated, knew he yearned for someone to give him pain with his pleasure and Holly was more than happy to do just that.

Climbing up his body to straddle him, she purposely didn't touch his straining cock and barely let her skin brush against his. She could feel the tension in his body and knew he would stay perfectly still for as long as she pleased. He wouldn't dare to try and touch her, not until she gave him permission. There was something intoxicatingly arousing about having a strong, muscular man beneath you and knowing you had complete control over him.

If she had more time, she'd draw this out until they were both to the breaking point and couldn't stand it a moment longer, but she knew they were drawing near to their destination. She didn't have much longer and she wasn't willing to lose her chance just to tease them both, even if that tease would be enthrallingly torturous.

Finally, she settled against him, gently rocking her hips so her warm wetness slid up and down the length of his cock. Grey's breathing turned choppy and his hands fisted against the seat at his sides, but he never broke eye contact, never hid the naked longing and adoration shining out at her, and never moved to touch her.

"Are you mine, Grey?" she asked softly.

"Yes," he moaned. "Yours, all yours Holliarepzus."

Her name on his lips stripped her of her composure, inflamed her to such a degree that she felt her glamour slip. For a single heartbeat, she accidentally revealed her true form, letting him see her as she really was. The green eyes that glowed with an inhuman fire, the red hair that sparkled like tinsel, the skin as pale as fresh snow, and the thick, black ram horns that sprouted from above her temples and spiraled back behind her head appeared for a split-second before she regained control and drew her glamour back over her like a veil.

Whipping a look over her shoulder to see if the other two noticed her slip, she found them busy redressing, unaware of the truth she'd just displayed. Turning back to Grey, she saw the fear and awe on his face and knew he'd seen. She narrowed her eyes and tensed, expecting him to try and get out from under her so he could escape from the *monster*. But, just as he surprised her in the alleyway, he did so again.

"Beautiful," he breathed, raising his hand to touch the side of her head where her horns had been a moment ago.

He wouldn't feel anything. She was a higher demon and her magic was strong, but that he wanted to touch them at all was enough to make her shriveled heart swell.

Darting forward, she kissed him hard, lifting up at the same time to reach between their bodies and position him at her entrance. She sank down bit by bit, relishing the feel of him stretching her and rewarding him for his reaction.

Sliding up just as slowly, Holly set a deliberate pace, one that had them both moaning continuously. She rose up gradually, clenching her walls tightly, then dropped down hard, taking all of him.

She drove both of them crazy with the agonizingly slow climb to release, but it was worth every maddening second. They hit their peaks together, gasping and straining against each other as he filled her, and she convulsed around his thick, pulsing cock.

He opened himself to her while she rode him, giving her every dark, broken shred of his soul, and in return he showed her he was unafraid, undaunted by her inhuman-ness. She could feel his intensity, could almost touch the devotion bordering on obsession he had for her, and knew she wouldn't be able to let him go. She wouldn't be able to let any of them go. She'd been fooling herself to think she could take these memories and be satisfied.

Holly knew what she had to do.

She would have to stand against the terror of the night, the devourer of souls, The Dark Clause, and ask him to grant her this favor—a favor no one had ever dared to ask.

CHAPTER SIX

Holly fell against Grey, breathless, still almost imperceptibly undulating her hips against him as she drew out every ounce of pleasure he had to give before finally going still.

She felt sated now after taking all three of them and resolved in what she needed to do.

After giving Grey a tender kiss, she climbed off of him and redressed, gesturing for him to do the same.

He joined her when she moved to sit between Vien and Nash, taking his place at her feet and relaxing back against her legs. Holly carded her fingers through his hair and leaned her head on Vien's shoulder while she gazed out the window. They'd be arriving any moment.

When Grog pulled up in front of the hotel and came to a stop, they all exited, Nash reaching back to offer her a hand. She let them gawk at the towering building for a moment before ushering them inside.

The Pilazza was one of the most expensive and sought-after hotels in the entire city. Unfortunately for the humans who wanted to stay there that night, the entire hotel was rented out for Krampus' festivities. Any who tried to enter suddenly had the urge to check out a different hotel.

The Pilazza was decked out in all the best Christmas decorations. There were enormous garlands strung across the expanse of the building, thousands upon thousands of glittering white lights streaming from window to window, and numerous Christmas trees lining the lobby. Each tree was decked out in delicate glass ornaments, tinsel, and bows.

Only the best for their coming master.

"This is where the party is?" Nash asked, a bit of awe softening his usually clipped voice.

"Only the best for my boss," Holly replied, repeating what she'd only just said in her head.

"And who is the boss?" Vien questioned, suspicion bleeding from him.

Holly looked over at them, only to see all three were staring at her curiously. She was normally supposed to give the human prey some spiel about a billionaire CEO who ran the parties but, at this point, she didn't see the point in lying to them.

She took in a deep breath, and just gave them the truth. "Krampus, my master."

Three sets of eyes widened in disbelief at her words.

"As in… the opposite of Santa?" Grey asked slowly.

The look on his face was less doubtful and more wary than she expected. It was as if he wanted to not believe her, but after seeing a flash of her true form in the car he was having trouble dismissing her statement as a joke.

Holly bit her lip and nodded. Had she just made a huge mistake?

"So... if Krampus is real, does that mean Santa is too?"

Grey asked the first question that popped into his mind. He was having a hard time processing this. It all seemed so far-fetched, but at the same time, he somehow knew she wasn't lying to them. Her expression was serious, and her eyes held nothing but genuine honesty.

After seeing her change right in front of his eyes, seeing her become something otherworldly and so beautiful it made his heart skip, he knew he couldn't dismiss anything anymore.

Holly felt her lip curl at his question. "We don't talk about... *him*."

Why does everybody care about that blundering fool?

"Why not?" Vien asked quietly, his heart beating a little faster in his chest as he awaited her answer.

He wanted to brush off her words as make-believe, but his gut told him she was telling the truth and he always trusted his gut. It had saved his life more times than he could count.

He felt like he was losing his mind, but hadn't he

known from the second he saw her that she was different? She called to him in a way no one ever had, drew him to her like a siren. He felt the tether connecting him to her and through it knew she spoke true.

No matter how crazy it sounded or how much he wanted to disregard her statement, he couldn't. It was absolutely crazy, but he trusted her. For the first time *ever*, he trusted someone.

HOLLY WATCHED THEM CLOSELY AS SHE SPOKE, SEARCHING their expressions for any hint of doubt or disbelief.

"When St. Nick was born into the world, another power was born alongside him. Santa is pure joy and goodness, but it was too much. The world can't have all good. Everything has to have a balance. Krampus brought that balance. Every year, for one night, he devours the evil and sad souls that either deserve or want to leave this world behind. Their souls preserve his magic, the magic of all his legion, and the underworld where we all live. Santa does his thing, pushing back any excess darkness left over and sets the balance. Neither can live if the other dies. Both have the same limit of power and cannot destroy each other either. That's about the gist of it."

The men looked at each other, then back at her. Nash was the one to voice the realization she could see in all their eyes.

"So that makes you a... demon."

"Yes."

CHAPTER SEVEN

❄

*B*efore the men could ask any more questions, they were interrupted by a lower demon approaching them. Not wanting to arouse suspicion, Holly subtly nodded her head, telling them to go with it. She knew they would be ushered to one of the hotel rooms for a change of clothes.

Anxious to have them back with her, Holly hurried to her own room and quickly slipped into the black, silk dress she'd picked out for the festivities. The low neckline dipped down to her navel and the material clung to her, hugging and accentuating her curves perfectly. She slipped on some black pumps to match and walked out of her room in time to see the men being escorted from theirs by the lowers.

They all looked devilishly handsome in matching black tuxedos—even Grey looked like a whole new man. She knew what he'd been hiding under that oversized shirt, but seeing him now all decked out made her want to drag him to a dark corner and strip it right back off. His hair had been pushed backed and combed, accentuating his square jaw and handsome features.

Nash looked uncomfortable in the suit but wore it like he was made for it. Vien looked just as imposing in his as he did in his casual attire. To say they were all mouthwatering was an absolute understatement.

Holly stopped in the middle of the hallway, pulling their attention from eyeing the lower who, like Grug, wore an ill-fitting skin suit. When their gazes landed on her, their jaws dropped in tandem. Smirking, she cocked a hip and tossed her hair.

"You like?" she asked in a sultry voice.

When they nodded wordlessly, she laughed lightly and dropped the pose, holding her arms out for the men to grab.

Vien chose to walk behind as Grey and Nash looped her hands through their elbows. Holly lead them back down to the ballroom on the first floor, ready to get the night started.

The room was full of people when they walked in. Demons, dressed in their best ensemble, strolled around the massive space, parading their human prey, showing off their selections for the night's sacrifice. The humans were none the wiser of what was going to happen to them and were celebrating with champagne and food.

Dark instrumental Christmas music filtered through the glittering room, setting the mood for the night. The black floor was polished to such a shine it reflected the lights from the towering, blood red Christmas tree that sat at the back of the room. It stretched at least sixteen feet high, leaving only a few feet between it and the ceiling, and was adorned with white lights, silver snowflakes, and black tinsel.

Holly loved when the demons gave Christmas decor a dark twist. The lobby decorations reflected the norm for what the humans outside expected to see, but the decor in this room, hidden away from the large windows of the lobby, reflected the much darker side of the holiday that Krampus' demons appreciated.

"The party has started, and we have maybe fifteen minutes until midnight. You three ready to mingle for a bit?" Holly asked.

They all nodded but said nothing as they took in the ominously beautiful view. Holly could feel their wariness, but an underlying sense of acceptance seemed to hum between the three of them. They were nervous, but they trusted her and were ready for whatever awaited them.

She looked at them for a moment, debating whether she should tell them what would happen at midnight, but decided against it. Just in case Krampus didn't grant her wish, she didn't want to fill them with false hope. Better they enjoyed themselves.

Holly led them through the crowd, occasionally getting a nod from some of the other high-level demons as they passed. She could hear a few whispers about her, her brethren noting she'd brought two more humans than necessary. Most high-level demons only brought one sacrifice. Holly generally liked upping the odds, but this time she hoped her show of devotion to Krampus would soften him and up her chances of getting what she wanted.

They'd just grabbed a flute of champagne each, when a

lilting voice called her name. She groaned under her breath when she recognized the female, and turned slowly to face her, her expression settling into a moue of distaste.

"Settia," Holly greeted in a droll tone, downing her champagne in the vain hope that it would make the coming conversation more tolerable.

Settia—or Poinsettia, her demon name—was Holly's longtime nemesis. The two of them had been feuding for centuries. Settia had always hated that Holly was Krampus' favorite and spent many decades trying to sabotage her close relationship with their master. She'd gone so far as to try and steal Holly's victims before she could seal the deal with bringing them. Her viciousness was unrivaled, and her jealousy more so. She was desperation in its most pure form.

"My, my. Look what you've brought this year," Settia purred, eyeing the guys surrounding Holly with rapt interest.

She slid her hands seductively up her blood red, silk gown—one that looked exactly like Holly's, if in a different color—doing her best to catch the men's attention.

Her eyes were black as night, her equally black hair was cut in a short bob, and her lips were painted a glittering gold, but where Holly was curvaceous and lush, Settia was so thin she bordered on emaciated. Her gaunt frame was a side effect of not having Krampus' favor. Everyone knew the joy their master received from starving her of energy in their dominion, but what they didn't know was that it was at Holly's behest.

Settia purred under breath when her gaze landed on

Vien. She drew in a deep breath and stepped closer to him, the look on her face starved and desirous.

"Oh, he smells divine. The violence rolling off him tastes delectable," she breathed. Cutting her dark eyes to Holly she asked eagerly, "You wouldn't happen to want to part with that one, would you?"

Holly stepped forward, blocking Settia from moving any closer.

"I think not. These are mine," Holly clipped warningly.

Settia chuckled scornfully, hiding her disappointment behind a sneer, then looked between Nash and Grey assessingly.

"Well, at least two of them seem to be worth it, but this one," she motioned at Grey, "this one is just pathetic and so... *average*."

Holly felt a pang come from Grey. Anger, swift and murderous, burned through her at the insult. She growled deep in her throat and felt her composure slip. Without a doubt, her glamour had come undone. Her twisted horns appeared menacingly on either side of her head, and she felt her eyes grow hot with glowing green fire that promised violence.

"He is *mine*. You will keep your comments to yourself Settia, or I will happily tear the pound of flesh from your body that I've been salivating for since the beginning."

Settia's eyes seemed to dim a bit in fear, but she quickly regained her composure and straightened.

"No need to get your tinsel in a tangle, Holly. I was only observing," Settia huffed and began to walk around them.

Holly pivoted with her, tracking her with her eyes. She

knew Settia wouldn't give up so easily and was ready to strike if she tried anything, watching her hands closely. Where Holly could enthrall her prey without touch, Settia wasn't powerful enough for that. She needed to touch her victims to bring them under her spell.

As predicted, Settia went to stretch out a hand and touch Vien as she passed. It was a mistake, and one that Settia learned quickly, but not because of anything Holly did.

It was Vien that stopped her touch from landing.

CHAPTER EIGHT

❄

When Settia's hand came close, Vien, quick as a snake, pulled a knife from seemingly thin air and slashed at her palm. He cut deep, sending a spray of black blood arcing through the air to land with a hiss on the polished floor. Settia reeled back with a vicious hiss, cradling her hand to her chest and staining her red gown with the inky fluid.

"You fucking skin sack!" she shrieked.

Her own glamour dropped, revealing her pale grey, deformed horns, warped and misshapen where they sprouted from her temples. She bared her jagged teeth at Vien and lunged forward, her intentions to tear him to shreds clear. Vien tensed, his lips curling into a cold, anticipatory grin, but this time it was Holly's turn to teach Settia a lesson.

Holly didn't miss a beat. In the span of a blink, she was in front of Settia, grabbing her by the column of her throat and lifting until her feet left the floor. She clawed at Holly's hand, kicking her feet and making helpless choking sounds, but her struggles were ineffective.

"I warned you! Did you think I would let your insolence go unpunished?" Holly roared, giving Settia's neck a good squeeze to emphasize her point, digging her nails in until warm blood ran over her hand.

No matter how much Settia wished it, she would never be even half the demon Holly was. That she'd dared to try and steal one of her men meant Holly needed to put her back in her place. As soon as they returned to the underworld, she would do exactly that but, for now, she would bide her time. The humans were staring and there was only so much fear their keepers could calm.

"If you try my patience again, I won't worry about the humans. I'll gut you where you stand and watch you choke to death on your own blood then dance in your entrails. Understood?"

Settia nodded quickly, her face a delightful shade of purple and her eyes bulging in their sockets.

Holly dropped her, smirking when she stumbled and coughed violently, then said sweetly, "Good girl. Run along, now. Krampus comes soon."

Settia said nothing else as she hastily staggered away. The room—which had fallen silent at the spectacle—became loud once more as though nothing had happened, her demon brethren taking quick measures to pull their victims back under their influence, so they didn't panic at the sight of two demons fighting.

When Holly felt the presence of her men behind her, her victorious smile quickly fell. With a sniff, she knew instantly that all of her previous pheromones had slipped away, leaving them completely coherent. She also realized her glamour was still gone, showing off her demonic features in full fashion. Grey had seen her for just a second, but the other two hadn't. How would they react to her true form? Would they be horrified? Usually she reveled in the fear of humans, but the possibility of seeing that on her men made her chest tight.

She turned slowly, ready to face expressions of revulsion and terror from them, but when she raised her gaze, she found neither. Instead, she found desire blazing in their eyes.

"That was the sexiest thing I've ever seen," Vien rasped lowly, his heart pounding with the need to touch her.

He didn't know what she was, but he knew he wanted her more than he had just five minutes ago, which he hadn't thought possible. He'd fantasized about finding a woman who loved violence as he did, who had their own monster locked away inside them, but resigned himself long ago to never finding such a person. Clearly, he'd been wrong.

The look of fury and bloodlust on her beautiful face, the demonic horns that appeared on her head, the green glow that ignited in her eyes, illuminating a soul just as dark and twisted as his own, made him want the dazzling creature standing before him more than ever. What had already been desire and adoration turned to fanatical obsession in an instant.

Vien knew, without doubt or reservation, that he would walk through hell to keep her.

NASH CLENCHED HIS FISTS TO STOP HIMSELF FROM grabbing Holly. He knew what he'd just witnessed should scare him. The sight of her turning into something that was obviously not human should send him running as far away from her as quickly as possible.

But that wasn't what he wanted at all.

He wanted to grab those striking horns and use them to hold her in place while he fucked her from behind. He wanted to feel the edge of the fangs he'd seen past her red lips scraping over his neck as she rode him. He wanted to stare into those luminous eyes until he knew all her secrets.

For the first time since he'd killed his wife that horrible night so many years ago, Nash felt alive. The numbness he'd lived in for so long fell away completely, pushed aside by the ferocity of emotion that flooded him.

Holly was his and he was hers.

GREY FELT THE SAME AWE AND REVERENCE HE'D FELT IN THE car come back ten-fold. She was glorious. In the time between then and now, he'd almost convinced himself that what he'd seen when she was poised above him wasn't real. A being so darkly magnificent and other-worldly couldn't possibly exist, but she did. He knew he should be terrified. Facing the reality of demons and magic, learning that Krampus was real, should horrify him. Yet, all he felt was captivated.

Seeing Holly so angry and violent should scare him, but it didn't. She was beautiful in her fury and her violence drew him to her. No matter what his ex-wife wanted, he'd never been the dominant type. He'd always secretly craved a woman who would take him, control him, and give him the pain he needed with his pleasure.

Holly was that woman and Grey would do anything it took to be hers.

CHAPTER NINE

❄

*H*olly tasted their emotions on the air, felt them suffusing her in a warm rush. Exhaling sharply at the relief that spread through her, she stepped into them, rejoicing in their touch as they crowded close and stroked her skin.

Something happened as they embraced her. With her glamour still off and her guard down, she unintentionally let part of herself slip into them.

Instead of seeing their lives, they saw hers.

She started to pull away, but their hands stopped her. They held her in place, not letting her break the connection. A miniscule frisson of hope prevented her from fighting to be free. The possibility, however small, that they would accept her froze her feet in place.

Taking a deep breath, she allowed the wall fall away and let them in completely.

She saw it with them, experienced the centuries she'd lived in rapid succession. Blood, pain, loneliness, the time spent between the yearly hunt for sacrifices in the under-world, Krampus, the relish she felt for luring in her victims, and the pride she felt when they jumped willingly into The Pit to power their dimension for another year.

All of it flashed through them. Every dark, depraved act, every victim she'd killed was there for them to see. The forlorn desolation that had been building inside her for decades that she'd hidden from everyone, even herself, was revealed to them. And, finally, under the dark, twisted parts, the tiny spark of love that had somehow managed to survive all that wickedness grew bigger and bigger when she felt their reaction to her life.

They saw her in all her dreadful glory... and they accepted her.

Holly felt the bond she'd created between them solid-ify. She felt their souls mesh with hers, felt them snake through her being until she couldn't tell where she started, and they ended.

They stood there for endless minutes, lost in each other... until the clock struck twelve.

The last chime was immediately followed by a great tearing sound coming from behind them.

"He's here," she gasped, pulling away from their touch and blinking open her eyes.

Spinning around, she saw a portal opening in the middle of the ballroom floor. From the edges, darkness spilled out, bringing with it the smell of blood-soaked sugar cookies, roasting flesh, and cloves. The scents brought a smile to Holly's lips.

Home.

As soon as the portal was fully open, people began walking toward it. Humans, their eyes glittering with the twinkle of black Christmas lights and dazed but eager smiles stretching their mouths, shuffled to their deaths happily while their demon hosts clasped their hands and watched the show with joy and pride.

This was why Krampus' demons only chose corrupt, sad souls who were ready to let go of this world. They needed no provocation. They didn't have to be pushed to their deaths. The magic of their master seeped into them readily and called them to him.

Holly flicked her gaze to the men on either side of her, worried for a moment that they, too, would try to walk to the hole, but they stayed right where they were.

Vien turned his head to meet her gaze, then gave her a wink. Nash settled a hand at the nape of her neck, and Grey stepped closer to run his fingers over the back of her arm. She hadn't known if they would feel her emotions as she did theirs, but they obviously did and immediately moved to reassure her.

When the last of the mediocre sacrifices fell—the demons hoping to gain favor with particularly corrupt victims holding their sacrifices back—a thick, cloying mist arose. From within it came the tips of a huge rack of black horns, growing larger and larger as Krampus emerged.

He hovered a moment, letting his legion bask in his hideous magnificence. His horns rose above his head like a gnarled crown. His back, arched in an impossible hump, was cloaked with a tattered, black, fur-lined robe adorned with the bones of his favorite victims. Draped over his bent arms were lengths of chain, decorated with bells that tinkled ominously with every movement.

The thump of his cloven feet stepping onto the polished floor echoed through the room, sending an expectant hush over those present. He turned his great head and fixed his fathomless eyes on her. Holly held a staying hand out to her men and approached.

Coming to a halt less than two feet away, she tipped her head back and smiled hopefully up at him.

"Hello, my Master," she beamed, her nervousness outshined by the childlike wonder she always felt in his presence.

Krampus hooked a terrifyingly long, bony, claw-tipped finger under her chin and stared down at her with eyes that held horrors beyond imagining. Holly felt a cold slithering touch brush against her mind and opened herself to him, letting him see all she'd done that night.

After a minute, he withdrew his touch from her mind, leaving her shaky and cold.

"I like them," she whispered, gazing up at him pleadingly. "May I keep them? Pretty please? I'll take such good care of them, and next year, I'll bring you the tastiest, most evil souls."

His chuckle was the thing of nightmares, grating and rasping, and his smile was monstrous. Holly could feel the fear coming from everyone behind her, including her men, but she was focused on Krampus, heart pounding with anticipation as she waited for his answer.

"Yessss, my treasure. You may keep them, but you

know the rules. They must be remade as one of mine. Only demons can live in our world," he rasped.

Holly squealed and darted forward, hugging him tightly. She felt his claws brush over her head, before she let go and strode back to her men.

Smiling hopefully, she held her hands out, leaving the final decision up to them.

Grey was the first to accept, sliding his fingers into hers and moving to stand at her side.

Nash glanced at Krampus behind her, currently devouring the remaining sacrifices held back for him, then met her eyes. He smiled and took her other hand, leaving Vien the last to decide if he would join her as a demon and face the centuries at her side.

She could feel that he wanted to say yes, but something was holding him back.

"What is it, my Monster?"

"Will I still get to kill people?" he asked with a sly smile.

Holly threw her head back and laughed in delight. "As often as you'd like, my love. If you're bad enough, Krampus might even let you help me hunt next Christmas."

"Sounds perfect, my *koroleva*," Vien replied, leaning forward to kiss her softly.

Holly took one last look at all three of them, before tightening her grip.

"Close your eyes and hold your breath," she told them.

When they did as she said, she pulled them with her, plunging them over the edge and into the portal. As the air rushed past, surrounding them with the comforting smell of cloves, blood-soaked cookies, and roasting flesh, Holly grinned, knowing she would never be alone again.

Grey, Nash, and Vien were the best Christmas present a demon could ask for.

THE END

We wish you all a very merry Christmas, and remember, be nice, for it's not Santa that checks the naughty list ;)

"During Christmas, open your heart with love to appreciate the beauty of life and all the presents that you have received from the earth."
—Debasish Mridha

ABOUT THE AUTHOR

About Stacy Jones

Stacy Jones is an award-winning author with an obsession for all things science fiction, romance, and adventure. She adores creating strange, wondrous worlds and watching her characters come to life.
She can usually be found typing frantically on her laptop, dancing like a crazy person with her son, or cuddling with her husband.
To learn more and be the first to know of upcoming releases, news, and events, follow her here…

Website
www.stacyjonesauthor.com

Newsletter
http://bit.ly/stacyjonesauthornewsletter

Social Media
https://linktr.ee/stacyjonesauthor

Facebook Page
https://www.facebook.com/stacyjonesauthor

Facebook Fan Group
https://www.facebook.com/groups/728238767375518

Instagram
https://instagram.com/stacyjonesauthor

Amazon
https://www.amazon.com/Stacy-Jones/e/B078HWPVY1

Goodreads
https://www.goodreads.com/author/show/
17528787.Stacy_Jones

BookBub
https://www.bookbub.com/profile/stacy-jones

More By Stacy Jones

Chosen Series

Chosen: Book One

http://books2read.com/u/bzPZd2

One minute Lily is trying, and failing, to run her grandmother's farm—her last remaining connection to her family. The next, she wakes to find herself in a cold, sterile cage surrounded by monsters, with no memory of how she got there. Accidentally abducted by alien poachers, unsure if she will live or die, she is dreading the worst. What she doesn't expect is for her captors to dump her on an alien planet, leaving her to fend for herself. Now, she must fight to survive the planet... or die trying.

Frrar, Tor, and Arruk have been Searching endlessly for a mate to belong to, someone to finally accept them, but they are losing hope. The time of cleansing, when the great waters drown the land, draws near. They are on the verge of abandoning their search and fleeing the forest when they spot a strange, tiny, two-armed female. They are immediately drawn to her, fascinated by her differences, but they must act fast to save her life, and their own, from the coming flood.

Tribe Outsider: Book Two

http://books2read.com/u/47ZQOL

Despite being dumped on a primitive alien world, Lily is adapting to life there, with the help of Frrar, Tor, and Arruk. But they can't stay in the safety of the caves forever. The flood waters have receded and it's time to join the rest of the tribe…

While traveling, their group meets a familiar face from Arruk's past – a man half feral and covered in vicious scars. Something about him draws Lily in, despite those who already hold her heart. But that isn't her biggest concern.

Can Lily keep the Tribe Mother from discovering just how much being with her has changed her new mates? Will the tribe accept her, a stranger in their lands? Or will Lily have to fight the very people who were supposed to offer her safety and a home?

Tribe Protector: Book Three

http://books2read.com/u/b62oMW

Lily thought she had her hands full with her conflicted feelings over her quickly progressing relationship with Arruk's wild twin, Drrak, the uneasy truce with the tribe leader, and trying to prove she's trustworthy to a people who want nothing to do with her. But all that pales in comparison to what's coming.

When Lily and her mates are sent into the forest to investigate the intruders closing in on tribe territory, they find something so horrifying it shocks Lily to her very core. But more than that, it pisses her off.

Driven now by the need to protect a people not her own and to stop the monsters that hunt them, Lily gathers the tribe to her cause, enlisting them to help her. But will they be ready in time or will Lily lose everything in the fight for survival?

❄

Khargals of Duras Series Book One (Multi-Author Series)

Gravel and Grit by Stacy Jones

<u>My Book</u>

Zaek is losing hope after waiting centuries for rescue, but the time has finally arrived. The lost emergency beacon has fallen from orbit and gone active. All he needs to do to get off this damn planet named Earth is find it and get to the pick-up location in time. The problem? The beacon comes with an addictively confounding, Earthian female who makes his mating gland swell, marking her as his true mate. Zaek hasn't been around a human who didn't run away screaming monster in a millennium, so how the hell is he supposed to convince this smart, beautiful, sarcastic female to give him the opportunity to win her heart before he loses his chance forever?

Mira has always been obsessed with all things alien, but when one breaks into her lab at Area 51, first contact doesn't go how she planned. Kidnapped and running for her life with a gruff gargoyle that definitely isn't made of stone and has more than his share of quirks, Mira learns that sometimes plans are made to be thrown out the window.

With a black ops team hot on their heels, determined to kill or capture them both, time is running out and their fumbling romance isn't the only thing standing in their way to happiness.

Hard as Rock By Stephanie West (Khargals of Duras Book 2)

Heart of Stone by Regine Able (Khargals of Duras Book 3)

Sticks and Stones by Tamsin Ley (Khargals of Duras Book 4)

Etched in Stone by Abigail Myst (Khargals of Duras Book 5)

Taken for Granite by Nancey Cummings (Khargals of Duras Book 6)

Rock my World by Zara Zenia (Khargals of Duras Book 7)

My Book

A KISS OF MADNESS BY STACY JONES AND K.B. EVERLY

My Book
I've always known things I shouldn't know and seen things I shouldn't see. One terrifying vision—and my reaction to it—lands me in Brocker's Center for the Criminally Insane.

I'm convinced I can survive my time here unscathed. After all, I'm not crazy. But after spending time with three guys—a schizophrenic with two personalities, a pathological liar who can't be trusted, and a nymphomaniac with a penchant for knives—I'm beginning to doubt my sanity.

Can I separate the real from the mad, or will this place make me spiral further down into the dark recesses of my mind?

Am I crazy?
I'll let you decide…

This is a dark romance novel that'll leave you questioning if what you're reading is true, or just a Kiss Of Madness

Hyde With Me by Stacy Jones and K.B. Everly
My Book
What would you do to save the life of someone you love?

Jaquelyn Hyde, chemical pathologist student, asked herself that question many times as she fought to find a cure for the disease slowly killing her aunt and could only ever come up with one answer.

Anything.

But she quickly realizes getting what you want comes with a price... and that price can be higher than you're able to pay.

This REVERSE HAREM Urban Fantasy will show you what happens when the monsters don't stay in the closet... but lie in wait within ourselves.

Saving Merritt by Stacy Jones and CoraLee June
My Book
My dad, a small town detective, died last month, but I stopped knowing him over a decade ago when he sent me away. So, I was surprised to learn that he left me everything—including his retired K9 dog, Remy.

Determined to claim Remy and return to my life in Nashville, I wasn't prepared to see them again.

My best friends. My first loves.

Denver, the sweet but fierce K9 officer with guilt in his eyes. Tatum, the reclusive mountain man next door, hellbent on making me keep my father's land. And Krew, my charismatic friend, now an unlikely member of a dangerous motorcycle club.

I assumed they forgot about me, but they haven't. I thought I was over them, but I wasn't.

The innocence of childhood love turns deadly when secrets are revealed. I've learned more about the father I thought didn't want me, but that knowledge? It may very well get me killed.

ABOUT THE AUTHOR

About K.B. Everly

K.B. Everly is a USA Today Bestselling author from Southern Mississippi. She has one daughter, a pup, and two cats who she claims are stealing her soul in only tiny doses, so she won't notice. She can be found (or not found) hiding from her tiny human so she doesn't have to share her snacks. Usually it's in the closet. What free time she has is used fighting with Malegficent, her prosthetic leg, or stuffing her face with copious amounts of coffee and candy as she types away on her next book.

WEBSITE
www.kbeverlyauthor.com

FACEBOOK PAGE
www.facebook.com/KBEverlyAuthor

FACEBOOK GROUP
www.facebook.com/groups/1964019597163164

INSTAGRAM & TWITTER
@kbeverlyauthor

AMAZON

www.amazon.com/author/kbeverly

THE DIVINELY DAMNED SERIES

The Arbiter: Divinely Damned Book One

books2read.com/TheArbiter

STANDALONES

Suffer Less

books2read.com/SufferLess

Cruelty

books2read.com/Cruelty

A Kiss of Madness

books2read.com/Madness

The More the Merrier

books2read.com/TMTM

Polarity of Us

books2read.com/PolarityofUs

Printed in Great Britain
by Amazon

35696546R00040